A Note to Parents

Welcome to REAL KIDS READERS, a series of phonics-based books for children who are beginning to read. In the classroom, educators use phonics to teach children how to sound out unfamiliar words, providing a firm foundation for reading skills. At home, you can use REAL KIDS READERS to reinforce and build on that foundation, because the books follow the same basic phonic guidelines that children learn in school.

Of course the best way to help your child become a good reader is to make the experience fun—and REAL KIDS READERS do that, too. With their realistic story lines and lively characters, the books engage children's imaginations. With their clean design and sparkling photographs, they provide picture clues that help new readers decipher the text. The combination is sure to entertain young children and make them truly want to read.

REAL KIDS READERS have been developed at three distinct levels to make it easy for children to read at their own pace.

- LEVEL 1 is for children who are just beginning to read.
- LEVEL 2 is for children who can read with help.
- LEVEL 3 is for children who can read on their own.

A controlled vocabulary provides the framework at each level. Repetition, rhyme, and humor help increase word skills. Because children can understand the words and follow the stories, they quickly develop confidence. They go back to each book again and again, increasing their proficiency and sense of accomplishment, until they're ready to move on to the next level. The result is a rich and rewarding experience that will help them develop a lifelong love of reading.

For Raina
—A. S.

Special thanks to Little Eric, New York, NY,
for supplying shoes, and to Hanna Andersson, Portland, OR,
L.L. Bean, Freeport, ME, and Playclothes, Rio Rancho, NM,
for supplying shoes and clothing.

Produced by DWAI / Seventeenth Street Productions, Inc.

Library of Congress Cataloging-in-Publication Data

Schreiber, Ann.
    Shoes, shoes, shoes / by Ann Schreiber ; photography by Dorothy Handelman.
        p.   cm. — (Real kids readers. Level 2)
    Summary: A trip to a shoe store reveals an enormous variety of shoes.
    ISBN 0-7613-2004-0 (lib. bdg.). — ISBN 0-7613-2029-6 (pbk.)
    [1. Shoes—Fiction. 2. Stories in rhyme.] I. Handelman, Dorothy, ill. II. Title. III. Series.
PZ8.3.S3755Sh   1998
[E]—dc21   97-31374
                                                                                                  CIP
                                                                                                  AC

pbk: 10 9 8 7 6 5 4 3
lib: 10 9 8 7 6 5 4 3

Shoes, Shoes, Shoes

Anne Schreiber

Photographs by Dorothy Handelman

M

The Millbrook Press

Brookfield, Connecticut

Shoes, shoes, shoes, shoes.
So many kinds—
how can I choose?

Shoes with straps
and shoes with laces.
Shoes with holes in many places.

Shoes for running.
Shoes for walking.
Shoes for hanging out, just talking.

Some shoes are big.
Some shoes are tiny.
Brand-new shoes
are nice and shiny.

9

These are cool.
These are sweet.
These feel funny
on my feet.

10

These are soft
and very bright.
These come in both
black and white.

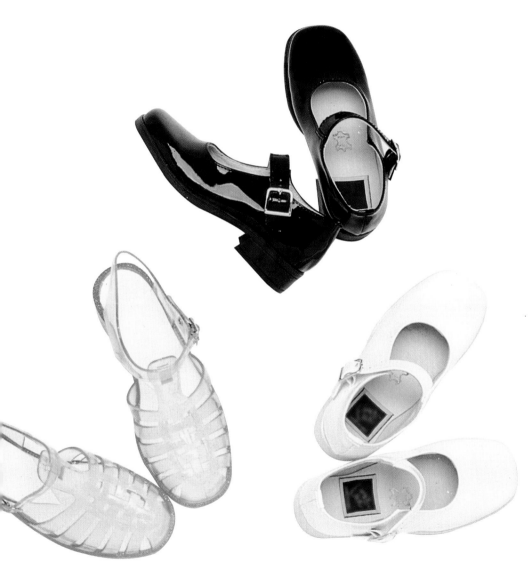

Shoes for games.
Shoes for sports,
like shooting hoops
out on the courts.

Shoes for swimming.
Shoes for rolling.
Silly-looking shoes
for bowling.

Tap, tap, tap, tap.
Tap shoes keep the beat.

And flip-flops are fun
in the sun and the heat.

When it rains and skies are gray,
these shoes let you splash and play.

When the snow falls from the sky,
these shoes keep you warm and dry.

Shoes, shoes, shoes, shoes.

So many kinds—
how can I choose?

I like high-tops.
He likes low-tops.

We both like
get-up-and-go tops.

21

Clean shoes.
Muddy shoes.

Green shoes.
Buddy shoes.

Shoes with heels
make us so tall.
But when we try to walk,
we fall!

We wear these shoes
when we play dress up,
but take them off
to clean the mess up.

Shoes with dots.
Shoes with bows.
These shoes pinch
my heels and toes.

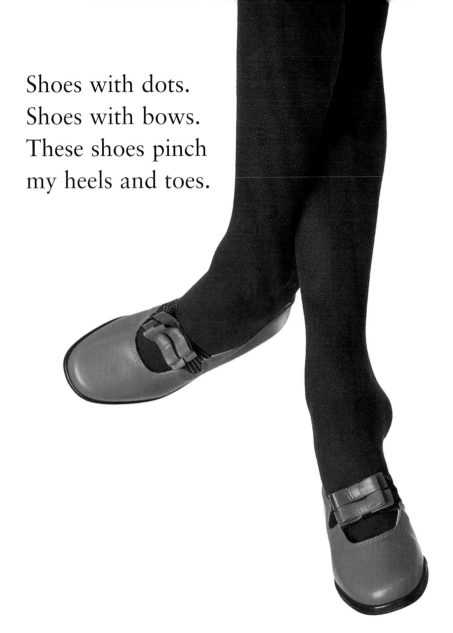

I don't like brown.
I don't want blue.
So many shoes—
what shall I do?

Wait! I found them.
Look at these!
They don't pinch
and they don't squeeze.

Green and white
and so much more.
They are the best shoes
in the store.

Shoes, shoes, shoes, shoes.

So many kinds—
which do *you* choose?

Phonic Guidelines

Use the following guidelines to help your child read the words in *Shoes, Shoes, Shoes*.

Short Vowels

When two consonants surround a vowel, the sound of the vowel is usually short. This means you pronounce *a* as in apple, *e* as in egg, *i* as in igloo, *o* as in octopus, and *u* as in umbrella. Short-vowel words in this story are: *big, but, can, dots, fun, get, let, tap, tops.*

Consonant Blends

When two or more different consonants are side by side, they usually blend to make a combined sound. In this story, words with consonant blends include: *best, black, brand, flip, flops, gray, just, soft, sports, straps.*

Double Consonants

When two identical consonants appear side by side, one of them is silent. Double-consonant words in this story include: *dress, mess,* and words in the *all* family: *fall, tall.*

R-Controlled Vowels

When a vowel is followed by the letter *r*, its sound is changed by the *r*. In this story, words with *r*-controlled vowels include: *are, for, more, sports, store, warm.*

Long Vowel and Silent E

If a word has a vowel and ends with an *e*, usually the vowel is long and the *e* is silent. Long vowels are pronounced the same way as their alphabet names. In this story, words with a long vowel and silent *e* include: *games, holes, laces, like, takes, places.*

Double Vowels

When two vowels are side by side, usually the first vowel is long and the second vowel is silent. Double-vowel words in this story include: *beat, clean, feet, gray, green, heat, heels, keep, play, rains, sweet, toes, wait.*

Diphthongs

Sometimes when two vowels (or a vowel and a consonant) are side by side, they combine to make a diphthong—a sound that is different from long or short vowel sounds. Diphthongs are: *au, aw, ew, oi, oy, ou, ow.* In this story, words with diphthongs are: *how, brown, new, out.*

Consonant Digraphs

Sometimes when two different consonants are side by side, they make a digraph that represents a single new sound. Consonant digraphs are: *ch, sh, th, wh.* In this story, words with digraphs include: *both, choose, much, pinch, shoes, these, they, what, when, which, white, with.*

Silent Consonants

Sometimes when two different consonants appear side by side, one of them is silent. In this story, words with silent consonants include: *talking, walking.*

Sight Words

Sight words are those words that a reader must learn to recognize immediately—by sight—instead of by sounding them out. They occur with high frequency in easy texts. Sight words not included in the above categories are: *and, at, come, from, funny, go, I, in, is, it, kinds, look, off, on, so, some, the, to, up, we, wear, you.*